Pink Moscato Diaries.

The Wine Glass Collection.

Nadine Hanley

NJS Books

ISBN: 0692667202
ISBN: 13: 978-0692667200

DEDICATION

This book is dedicated to all the sexual people, and who are sexually free when it comes to sex and your partner.

I would like to thank the man upstairs, my Lord Jesus Christ because he has given me so many talents to choose from and I am finally putting them to use.

Thank you for reading my book I truly hope you enjoy it. This book is for everyone who has sexual fantasies of some kind. Never hold your sexual frustrations in. Always be sexually free, in a safe way and with the one you love. And to my sister Tonya who has always told me that I could do it if I put my mind to it.

Much Love Nadine.

ACKNOWLEDGMENTS

ACKNOWLEDGMENTS

I would like to thank everyone who was involved in this process. And for putting up with me during this writing journey of mine.

I would also like to thank my husband Brian for being there for me when I needed you, and for supporting me through this new venture, and all of my other ventures that I have had. And helping me come up with new stories for this book and the next one in this collection...

Thank you and much Love Nadine.

Kandi

It was the week of my thirtieth birthday, and yet again I was without a date. My best friend Kannedy Jones, A.K.A Kandi was throwing me some kind of surprise girls night on Friday. I hoped the girls night involves male strippers. Me and Kannedy have been best friends since the third grade, she is more like a sister to me. But this bitch can get crazy when it comes to throwing parties. So I hope and pray it ain't wild; but then again I can use some wildness in my life. Kannedy has a lot of friends in the stripper, dancer world. She was once a stripper at one time, when we were in college, she did it to make extra money; that's where she got the name Kandi, from. But lately

I have noticed that when we are out together, people have the strangest look on their face when they see her, or say her name, it's like they are thinkin nasty thoughts about her. I asked her one day "why do people look at you that way when they call you Kandi." She laughed at me and said "cause my pussy tastes like candy." I looked at that bitch like she was crazy.

"So you telling me that all those damn females looking at you like that has tasted yo pussy?" Kannedy looked at me and smiled.

"Damn! You nasty bitch," I said. "Don't knock it until you try it," Kandi replied.

"Shit! I'm good on that Kannedy cause ain't no bitch goin down on me, and I sure as hell ain't goin down on no bitch. I'm Strictly Dickly." Kannedy laughed at me and said "sure, you right." But the thought of me getting

my pussy ate had me wet as hell. Now I don't know if the idea of a bitch doing it or a nigga doing it, is what got me wet. All I know is that it has been a long ass time since someone, anyone has been to my love cave. And I was hoping that I would have a man to share my birthday weekend with. So I could at least get me some birthday dick. But I was single as I wanted to be again. I just hope this party that Kannedy is throwing for me has some cute guys; at least some that I could maybe hook-up with later after the party, or some that have something going for himself. I don't think I'm bad looking, I'm 5'4, light skinned, with light brown eyes and long curly hair.

That belongs to me. Small waist, big ass, and nice D cup sized breast. And, I have a nice personality too. I actually think I'm a nice catch for someone special. Now my girl Kannedy has never had a problem getting men or women for that matter. She says that she doesn't go both ways, but hey if she like it, I love it. That's not gonna stop me from loving her like a sister. Because she will always be my bestie for life. Kannedy has a nice shape as well. She's 5'5, mixed her mom is black and her dad is white. Her ass is bigger than mine, with a tiny ass waist and a handful of boobs; hair down the middle of her back, with fucken green eyes, that she was born with.

Bitch knew she was cute, and used it to get what she wanted from men and women alike.

***Thursday** at work I received gifts and cards from my co-workers. I was so ready to clock out cause I took my birthday off which is Friday. I was so ready for tomorrow night, I hope my girl comes through and have some male dancers there and of course my fave, Pink Moscato. Shit I might stop at the store on my way home and pick me up a bottle or two, for tonight; while I get my bullet out and relieve some of this damn tension, and stress, before tomorrow night.*

As I went about my day at work, watching the clock for five o'clock to come, so I could clock out.

After work I stopped to pick up a few bottles of Pink Moscato. And headed home to have me a bomb ass orgasm with my bullet, because that seems to be the only way that this pussy was gonna see any action for my birthday, or any time for that matter. As I walk into my house, and into my living room. One of my favorite spots in the house, Because I have my sixty inch flat screen TV, mounted to the wall above my mantle, and below that I had twenty large square mirrors installed, with six round candle holders installed on each side of my mirrors, for those romantic nights. And next to my wall of mirrors nestled in a corner I have my stereo system and surround sound mounted in a corner shelf.

I walk over and light all twelve candles, and turn on my stereo system, the room comes alive with the smell of vanilla and black cherry fused together, and the sound of

Miguel singing The Pussy Is Mine', streaming throughout my house via the surround sound throughout my house. I walk into my chef's kitchen with the island in the middle of the floor that holds my counter top stove and my oven, I also have my double ovens mounted in the wall, as I walk towards my stainless steel double door refrigerator, I place the two bottles of wine in the freezer, to chill while I jump in the shower. As my play list of Miguel, R. Kelly, Maxwell, Janet Jackson, Adena Howard, Keith Sweat, and my girl, Jill Scott play throughout my house, I'm already in the mood, my pussy has started to get wet,

with just the thought of me touching myself.

Walking towards my bedroom to my master bath, I shed my clothes and toss them into the hamper. I grab my water proof bullet for the shower, and gather my other toys for when I get out. I check to make sure I have fresh batteries, because I hate being in the moment and my damn batteries die. As I step into my massive shower, that serves as a sauna as well. With dual shower heads, one on each end of the shower, perfect for when you have a man and you want to get busy in the shower. I turn on the water to hot and just stand there and let the water run down my body. I start touching myself, and fingering myself, feeling my pussy getting wet and juicy.

Squeezing my breast with my left hand while I pleasure myself with my right hand. Grinding on my hand I feel myself start to cum, but I don't want it to be over yet. I remove my fingers and taste myself, damn that shit is sweet.

I start to laugh out loud, thinking about my girl Kannedy who says her shit taste like candy. If that bitch could taste my pussy, she wouldn't know what to do, cause I know mines taste like candy. I reach over and grab my bullet from my little shelf in the shower. I sit on the stone shower bench and prop my legs up on the end of the bench, I let myself relax and I think of my pussy being played with, as I put my bullet to my clit feeling the vibrations, I close my eyes and I start to feel all these fingers just playing with my pussy at one time, making me wetter and wetter.

As I insert my bullet into my pussy I see my girl Kannedy's face in my head, she is in the shower with me kneeling down between my legs playing with my pussy, taking turns between her hands and her tongue. Kannedy was eating the fuck out of my pussy, making it drip with my juices. Damn if only this was not my imagination playing tricks on me. I begin to finger myself some more, I reach out the shower to my cabinet and pull out a ten inch dildo shaped like a dick, with a suction cup on the bottom. I attach it to the shower bench and proceed to ride that dick taking it all in. My pussy was so wet.

Damn why couldn't this be real; man... This pussy needed some TLC badly.

I began to lather my body with my favorite body gel, Simply Red, and the way my hands slide over my body made me wet all over again. I quickly rinse off, cause I was ready to get me a glass of Moscato and finish what I had started in the shower;
On the couch in front of my wall of mirrors After drying off I grabbed my toys off the bed that I had laid out prior to my shower.

Walking down the hall back to my front room with my birthday suit on, I pass the hall mirror and noticed how I looked, I smile at myself, because I loved looking at myself naked. I think I have a sexy body with curves in all the right places.

Continuing down the hall to the front room I stop in the kitchen to take out the wine I had placed there earlier, I put one in the fridge and open the other one and carry it to the front room and pour me some wine into the glass I had sitting on the end table. I was more relaxed with the aroma of my scented candles and my music playing, and of course with my wine. I placed a thick blanket down on my couch and settle down to have my ultimate orgasm: I gather my toys, I have my G-spot stimulator, my Jack rabbit, my bullet, my two headed dildo and my ten inch dildo shaped like a dick. Spreading my legs as I sit facing the wall of mirrors, I spread my pussy lips open and just touch myself, playing with my clit squeezing it, and sticking my fingers inside my pussy.

I watched as my pussy muscles contracted around my fingers making me more wet. I loved watching the way my pink pussy reacted to me touching it. I loved to see my juices running down my pussy. I pick up my bullet put it on full blast and place it on my clit, the sensation sent my head backwards and my eyes rolling to the back of my head. My pussy started to pulsate really fast, uncontrollably fast, I screamed out as my vajayjay gushed out all over the blanket. I thrust my Jack-rabbit into my pussy; my Jack-rabbit and my bullet going at my pussy at the same time, was making me so wet and slippery inside. My juices were coming out so fast that I had no control over it.

As the last wave of my orgasm washed over me, I felt myself coming down off of a high. The thrill of my pussy releasing all that it had to give was a feeling that I loved to have over and over. I finished off my bottle of wine as I sit in front of the mirrors playing with my love cave. A knock sounded at my door, and because I wasn't expecting anyone tonight I didn't bother to move from the pleasure that I was giving myself. I hear a key in the lock and I instantly remembered that Kannedy has a key to my place, like I do hers. I see Kannedy walk in, stop and look my way. "Girl! what are you doing?" She asked me as I sat there with my fingers in my love cave, and seeing Kannedy watching me made me feel bold.

I licked my lips as she stood there watching me like she wanted to help me play with this pussy. "What does it look like I'm doing, Kannedy?"

Kannedy licked her lips and moaned deep in her throat. "It looks like you need some help with that." She smiles at me, and for the first time I notice that she has two girls with her. I gasped, because I didn't notice them at first. Kannedy turns and looks at the other two girls standing slightly behind her and winks at them. They licked their lips as well, as they winked at me.

"We were coming over to see if you wanted to go get a drink, and go dancing at Jay's downtown, they have a live band tonight, but you seem to be drinking and enjoying yourself already."

Before I could get a chance to say anything, Kannedy tells the two girls to help me out. "Sparkle, Champagne go help Jessie out with that, she looks like she could use some help." The next thing I knew they were kneeling down in front of me, spreading my legs as far as they would go. One girl starts to lick my vajayjay while the other one squeezed my breast, and puts my nipple in her mouth, she bites my nipple sending shivers all over my body.

Damn! Damn!, that feels good," I moan. Closing my eyes and letting my head fall back to the top of my couch cushions, my vagina is throbbing something fierce. Damn this bitch knows how to eat some pussy. I look over at my girl Kannedy and she has somehow poured her a glass of wine from the unopened bottle in the fridge.

She was just sitting on the loveseat watching her friends Sparkle and Champagne, eat my pussy while she fingered herself. "lie on the floor baby girl."

One of the girls said, Sparkle, I believe. She is pretty, now that I look at her, long straight black hair to the middle of her back. She was thick with a nice body, nice ass and breast. Her skin is a dark chocolate complexion.

She was tall maybe five-eight or five-nine. The other girl, Champagne, was shorter around my height maybe a little taller than me, about five-six or so. She has a medium brown complexion, with a short and sassy haircut. She is more slender than the other girl. But she is still pretty.

I do what she says and lie down on the floor, I have no idea what is about to happen to me; but I'm loving the fact that my pussy is feeling lovely, and getting some action. The long haired girl, Sparkle, spreads my legs wide open and begins to finger me. She starts to talk to me softly as if she is trying to keep me from tensing up and keep me relaxed. She begins to tell me what is about to happen and what they wanted me to do. All I can do is nod my head okay. Again I look over to my girl, as if to get her permission to do this. She looks at me and winked. "It's ok Jessie, you're in good hands girl. Don't knock it until you try it, remember."

I nod my head again. I don't know what possessed me to do this, but a whole bottle of Pink Moscato has me with a real good ass buzz.

So I relaxed and let them do as they please to me. Sparkle sticks her tongue inside my pussy, I began to feel my vagina pulsating, she is sucking on my pussy lips so hard, but it feels so good at the same time. She lifts my legs up and licks me from front to back, while Champagne is sucking, and biting on my nipples, the sensation is awesome. Champagne sees my toys on the couch and gets my bullet and turns it on full blast and puts it to my clit, while Sparkle grabs my dick shaped dildo and begins to fuck me with it.

"Oh!Shit!"

I screamed as my pussy muscles started to contract harder and harder, and the vibrations from the bullet and her fucking me with the dildo sent me to another high; a high that I had never experienced before.

As she started to finger me and eat my pussy, like she is in love with it. I started to moan because this shit is the bomb, and I'm loving it. "Turn over and get on your knees." She tells me. I get on my knees, then Sparkle lies down in front of me, for me to eat from her honey pot, while Champagne eats mine from behind. I was nervous, because I have never in my life tasted another bitch's pussy.

Once I tried it, I was like damn that shit is good as fuck I couldn't stop eating and licking on. My pussy was dripping wet and this bitch was slurping on this pussy like she didn't want to miss a drop. The fact that it was different and that it involved two women, kept me wet and wanting more.

Kannedy was just watching and fingering herself like she wanted to join in, but not sure if she should or not. I didn't know that my pussy, or any pussy for that matter could cum so much. This went on for three hours. My shit was so swollen that I didn't think that I would be able to walk. But it was all worth it to me. I was spent, I had nothing left in me, my body was drained of everything.

lie on the floor breathing hard and trying to comprehend what had just happened. They helped me up off the floor and said "Jessica, you got some tasty ass pussy girl. We shall have to do this again." Kannedy looked at me as she sucked her juices from her fingers, and hugged me and said, "get some sleep girl you have a long day ahead of you tomorrow."

Champagne and Sparkle said bye in unison and walked out my house.

I was still reeling from the massive and multiple orgasms I had just had. I stumbled to my room, took a hot shower and fell asleep as soon as I hit the bed.

GIRLS NIGHT

Today is my birthday Girls Night and after last night I have no idea what my girl Kannedy has in store for me. I clean up my house from last night's pussy eating session, and get my house ready for my Girls Night.

Around seven-thirty that night the caterers started arriving to set up in my kitchen, for tonight. They didn't stay, they set up and then left. twenty minutes later more people started to arrive at my door. There were male strippers as well as female dancers. A pole was set up in the middle of my front room with disco lights and all. Kannedy and her crew came shortly after that. She had the two girls from last night,

Sparkle and Champagne, at her side and my pussy automatically started to get wet once seeing them. Kannedy was clad in a skimpy little see through black dress, that only covered her nipples and her crotch, with no panties on. Sparkle and Champagne were similarly dressed, Sparkle wore a red dress, and Champagne in a white dress. Kannedy had invited everyone that she knew to the party, that was fine with me because I had only invited a few people that I knew from work myself. As the show got started, and the dancers did their thing and food and wine was served, everyone was having a good time. Around two in the morning the guest began to leave. I was almost drunk from all the wine and drinks, that were being passed out, but it was the best party ever.

And I thought that was the end of the festivities, boy was I wrong. After everyone had finally left Kannedy and her two sidekicks stayed behind. "Happy birthday Jessie, I love you girl." Kannedy said as she gave me a hug and a kiss on the cheek. "Now the real fun begins," she said to me. I was confused because I thought we just had some real fun. But my girl Kannedy had other things in mind and I was about to find out just what that was. Now I never noticed her or her sidekicks bring in a big duffel bag full of shit; until she opened it up. "Now Jessie this is my birthday gift to you, I hope you enjoy it." Kannedy said smiling. "But first I must blindfold you." I wasn't sure about this at first, but this was my girl and I trusted her with my life. So she proceeded to blindfold me with a black cloth. and

immediately my other senses took over. I felt someone taking off my dress and my bra. I started to say something but someone put a finger to my lips, to stop me from speaking. "Just relax and enjoy the ride, this will be the best experience you will ever have, and I promise that you will enjoy every minute of it. And at any time that you want to stop just say the words." I nodded my head in understanding. All the while I was nervous and excited at the same time, because I didn't know what was about to happen.

But I was gonna trust my girl.

Someone spread my legs apart as I was standing there blindfolded, I felt hands on my ass and fingers inside my love cave, there was someone nibbling on my nipples, and running their hands all over my body. My legs started to give way and buckle on me, I wasn't able to stand there and take it any longer. Someone bent me over the side of the couch and spread my legs wide apart. I felt someone stick their tongue in my pussy from behind and all I could do was moan in pleasure. Sparkle spread my ass cheeks open and began to lick my ass, my pussy became wetter than ever before. This was new for me, but I didn't want to stop it, I was curious about it anyway.

Not saying that I like girls but somewhere in the back of my head I always wondered what it would be like to be with another woman. The next thing I knew I was on the floor with my hands tied above my head, and my legs spread so far open I thought they would break. I start to tense up because I felt a little fear set in, but Champagne whispered in my ear for me to relax, "nothing bad is gonna happen to you I promise, just take a deep breathe and relax, I promise Jessie you will love it." she said. She told me that they were gonna tie my legs just so they wouldn't move and so that I could get the full effects of all the pleasure they were going to be giving me.

I relaxed and let them tie me up. One started rubbing me down with a scented oil, while someone began to finger me and eating me at the same time.

I started to lick my lips and moan. I felt a nipple caressing my lips, I slowly open my mouth and place my tongue on her nipple, I was hesitant at first, but then I thought fuck it, who is gonna know about this, other than the people in this room... And I let myself go and get into the moment.

I began to nibble on her nipple and suck on it like it was a piece of candy, and I tell you I started to enjoy myself, And I was no longer afraid or nervous about what was about to take place in the privacy of my own home. I actually welcomed everything that they had planned for me. I felt something long, hard and warm going in and out of my pussy. It felt like a dick, but without the body attached to it.

As I felt her lady-juices on the inside of my leg, one of them had inserted a double headed dildo into my pussy and was fucking me with one end while they had the other end inside their love cave. As we both begin to grind on the double headed dildo our juices began to mix together, the feel of another woman's pussy touching mine is a feeling of new pleasure to me and it makes my love cave wetter and wetter. I feel someone pull my legs up in the air by a string of some kind, I feel one of them come between my legs from the front and lean over and eat my pussy, while someone lubes my ass up real good and penetrates my backdoor, now this is a different feeling for me also. Until now I was a virgin with anal sex. But damn it was a feeling I could get used to.

"Oh my gosh, this shit felt good," I say out loud.

Unbeknown to me my girl Kannedy is just watching all this go down between me and her two friends, Sparkle and Champagne. But she is enjoying the show herself. Suddenly Kannedy gets down on her knees and decides to join in on my fun. I never had thoughts of being with my best friend before, until a few days ago and I will never be the same after this night. Not sure if that is good or bad, but one thing for sure is that I am enjoying all the attention that my vajayjay is getting, after a long drought. Champagne sat her pussy in my face and for the second time in my life I tasted pussy, this shit was sweet as strawberries, I ate that shit like I was starving from hunger.

I slurped her juices from her like I was thirsty. My mind was going crazy, my pussy was so wet from all this stimulation at one time. I came so hard I thought I would have a heart attack. And Champagne's pussy tasted like strawberries. They took turns fucking me, touching me, licking me and doing shit that I never thought could be done... They poured wine all over my body and took turns licking it off, it ran down my stomach to my vajayjay and one of them lapped it up like a cat drinking milk from a bowl. They untied me so that I could touch them as well, they kept me blind folded so that I couldn't see who was who, I was ok with that.

Someone sat down on my face, she smelled so good, by this time I felt like I was good at eating pussy, I laughed to myself. Now this pussy was different it tasted different, felt different. This pussy was good and I thought, it tasted like a cherry starburst. How the hell does a pussy taste like candy? That shit was so damn good I was eating it like it was my last pack of starburst. Sucking on her clit and her pussy lips like I was a fucken pro. She rode my tongue like I was a master at pussy eating. All the while I was being ate out by one of the other girls.

I felt her cum all in my mouth as it ran down my chin. That made me cum at the same time. My pussy couldn't take no more.

But they weren't done with me yet, the one whose pussy tasted like candy turned around and started eating my pussy as she backed her ass and pussy onto my face so that I could continue to eat that pussy and her ass. Now mind you this is all new to me, but I'm loving it. They lift my legs up into the air again while I was still getting my pussy ate. They lube me up again and I feel them insert a dildo in my butt, she starts fucking me from the back and I cum so hard my juices were all over the floor.

I hear them all get up and leave me on the floor, Kannedy knelt down next to my face, "how did my pussy taste Jessica?" She whispered in my ear. "Like starburst," I said. She laughed and said. "Now you know why they call me Kandi."

She took the blindfold off, licked my pussy one last time as her sidekicks cleaned up the evidence of their girls night. I came one last time, before Kandi and her crew left. I will never be the same after this. She helped me up, hugged me and again wished me a happy birthday, and left.

Dear Diary, I will never be the same.

Jessie…..

Hello! Are you there?

Every night for the past week now someone has called my phone and not say anything. They just sit and breathe on the phone. So one Friday night they called again, this time I was ready for them.

"Hello!" I said in a soft sexy voice, are you there? The only response was heavy breathing. "Since you won't talk to me, then I'll talk to you.

"Hello! Are you there?" You know I was nervous at first when you started

calling me and wouldn't say anything, but then I figured you were just shy or something.

it started to turn me on, and I would sit here and play with myself until you called again. And I would wonder if you had a big dick or not. I love a man with a big dick; It makes my pussy sing.

Would you like for me to ride your dick for awhile? Spread my legs open so you can see it going in and out. Would you like that? Mmm mmm…. I start to moan.

Hello! Are you there? He starts breathing harder and harder. I start smiling cause I know I have him right where I want him. Close your eyes and just imagine that I am sliding up and down on that rock hard dick of yours.

As you watch my pussy get wetter and wetter. Look how your dick starts to glisten from all my lady-juices running down your shaft. Can you see it? Here let me put my finger inside my honey pot, and let you taste my sweet honey. Mmm mmm… don't that taste good? Here let me clean up my mess.

Can you feel my mouth wrapped around your love pole?

Can you feel how good it feels touching the back of my throat… Mmm… I can feel you pulsating in my mouth. No! No, don't cum yet. I'm not ready. Feel how I suck your pole from top to bottom, do you like it when I put your sac in my mouth?

Ooh, yeah.... You like it when I kiss you on your stomach, and lick you from top to bottom with the tip of my tongue, and sucking on your nipples, do you like that? Uh, ooh ooh... Mmm... I like it when you make me moan real loud. Can you feel the warmth of my wet pussy rubbing all up and down your stomach. I feel your hands all over my body as you spread my ass cheeks open and stick your finger deep inside my ass uh, mmm, yeah that's how I like it, deeper, deeper I whisper. My back is arched as you bite me on the ass and leave bite marks. Do you like the way my ass taste? Hello? Are you there?

Oh shit my pussy is throbbing really, really hard, can you feel it? Is this how you like it, with my ass in the air? You like eating this honey from the back, yeah I like that shit too... Mmm... Uh, Mmm, mmm, oooh yeees- Like that harder, harder, deeper. I love it when you fuck me hard and deep. Mmm... Uh yeah don't stop, I'm cumming (I scream). Yes, yes, yes- right there.

No, No, No don't cum, let me taste it...I love the way your cum taste... Uh, Mmm uh- You like it when I swallow don't you? Damn that was good.

Hello! Are you there?

I can still hear you, breathing. You must have loved it too. ***Click!***

The phone goes dead.

Hello! Are you there?

The Strawberry Bandit

I feel him touching me softly and I start to relax. I feel his mouth on my inner thigh, mmm… I start to moan, "I awake to my eyes being blindfolded and my arms tied above my head to my bed and my legs spread wide open, and also tied to the bed. My heart beat hard and fast wanting to scream but afraid no one would hear me. Then he whispers in my ear, "don't worry I won't hurt you. I'm here to please you. Just relax and go with the flow, believe me you will be glad I came." I tried to relax but the fear of the unknown was heavy in the air. The smell of him was intoxicating.

I know this scent from somewhere, but I can't put my finger on it.

"Who are you, and what do you want?" I ask him, he doesn't respond. I feel him put his mouth between my thighs, and softly kiss my treasure box, as he began to nibble on my love button. Damn that shit feels good, I want more, I say to myself. His tongue enters my pussy in and out like he was fucking me or something. I felt him start to finger me while he sucked and nibbled on my love button, making my pussy throb like crazy. "Can I tastes you?" I ask. I could tell that he wasn't expecting me to ask him that, but he slowly left my treasure box, and straddled my shoulders and put his thickness in my mouth. I moan out loud as I took him all in, massaging his dick with my lips and tongue.

I can tell he is enjoying it as much as I am. I deep throat his thickness, like it was the best thing I ever tasted, and actually it was. Not only did his dick taste good it smelled good too. I sucked the shit out of his thickness and made him cum so fast and hard. I could hear him breathing hard as fuck. I smile on the inside because, I know that whom ever this is he will be back for more.

I sucked him until I had all the cum that he had to give. Yes I swallowed it all. I could tell that he had been eating something sweet recently, like strawberries and pineapples, or something fruity; because his cum was oh so sweet and delicious. I licked my lips as I swallowed the last drop of his sweet nectar.

"I love the way your nectar taste, it taste like strawberries." I tell him. He gets up off me and starts eating from my honey pot again, until I began to climax, I came so hard. Never had I cum so hard before.

He bends over and whispers in my ear again "thank you so much I enjoyed your sweet pussy very much. Now go to sleep."

The next morning I woke up feeling like I had been fucked good the night before. It must have been a good ass dream I tell myself as I get up to get ready for work. Sitting on the side of the bed I notice a box and a note on my night stand.

"Thank you for a wonderful night.

The Strawberry Bandit."

Oh my gosh! Oh my gosh! I say out loud how the hell did he get in. Wait until I tell Ashley this, when I get to work. She is not gonna believe me. As I eat one of the strawberries from the box I start to remember the taste of his nectar in my mouth. And I smile to myself because I know for sure that he will be back sooner or later.

Sitting in my cubicle at work trying to get my computer screen to unfreeze, my friend Ashley asks me if I heard the news last night. It seems that the 'Strawberry Bandit' has struck again last night. Everyone has been talking about this guy like he is some kind of hero or something. I personally think he's awesome sneaking into women's houses and doing all kinds of sexual things to them, and leaving a box of chocolate covered strawberries next to their beds.

I block out what Ashley is saying about the 'Strawberry Bandit'. Because I have been sexually frustrated for the past year, after my boyfriend of four-years decided to walk away from my love. Not realizing that Ashley is still rambling on about the 'Strawberry Bandit', I look up to see Chad the computer tech guy walking past my cubicle.

"Chad! Chad!" I call out. Chad stops. "Yes, Ms. Dana, what can I do for you?" He asks as he walks back to my desk,

"can you please check out my computer it seems to be frozen." As Chad looks at my computer, Ashley continues to talk about the 'Strawberry Bandit'.

Something she says caught my attention. She said that bandit came to her place a few weeks ago. "So what did he do to you Ashley? And why are you just now telling me this?" I asked. She looked from me to Chad

and back again, "don't mind Chad he is not paying us any attention. Now spill the beans. " I said. Now I know this bitch is lying because this is something that she would have made sure that I knew about the moment it happened. And for her to wait two weeks, yeah she lying, I laugh to myself. She cleared her throat, "so tell me Ashley what happened."

I repeated , because I personally know what he is capable of doing, because he actually came to my house. I say to myself. I was going to tell this fool that, but no I'm gonna let her believe that I'm a fool, to think that he came to her house and did the things that he did to me, to her.

"Wow, Ashley I'm salty that he came to see you and not me." I say to her. Chad laughed to himself, at their conversation.

I could tell that she really thought that I believed that shit she was saying. I told her, "see if he came to see me I would suck his love pole and make him cum every time. I would fuck him so good that he wouldn't want to go sneaking into no other woman's window's. Shit he could do all that freaky shit to me." Chad's head popped up when he heard Dana say those things, because he really liked her, she was a very nice person and she was always nice to him. And she was cute too, that's why he made it a point to sneak into her house last night. But he wondered if she knew it was him. As Dana was talking to Ashley, she noticed that Chad was listening to everything they were saying. She smiled to herself, because she knew that he liked her, at least that's what the rumor is around the job.

Plus he's not so bad looking, She had a crush on him and has always wondered if he had a girlfriend or anything, but he always kept to himself, and he hardly ever spoke to anyone at the job. But she could see herself with him...

***Three nights later** she woke up blindfolded and tied to her bed, she smiled to herself; "I knew you would come back." I said to him. He bent down and whispered in my ear. "I loved the way your pussy tasted, and the way you sucked my dick, you are the only one who has done that to or for me. Everyone else just wants me to pleasure them." I feel him smile at me. "well, I like to pleasure as well as being pleasured. So before you begin can I taste you?"*

He bends closer and kisses me on the cheek, "yes, you can if you wish." "Yes I would like to." I say with a smile on my lips. He stands and undo his pants and removes them, he straddles me and proceeds to place his love pole in my mouth. "Mmm, Mmm... You taste so good," I said between sucking him, and licking his shaft. I heard him moan in pleasure, he was trying to keep his composure, but I had him where I wanted him. I say to myself if only he was my man. He had me thinking about Chad from work, if only... I start to enjoy this shit, as I suck his dick like it belongs to me. He starts to fuck my mouth this time, yes he is loving the way I massage this dick with my mouth. I feel him start to cum, I get ready for it to pour out into my mouth. He pulls out and cums on my chest and stomach.

"I want you to fuck me, if I untie you will you leave the blindfold on?" He asks. I nod my head yes, because I to want to feel that love pole inside my love cave. He slowly unties my hands and legs, he picks me up and sits on the the side of my bed and sits me on his dick with my legs wrapped around him. Damn this shit is good and hard. just the way I like it. I start to ride his dick long and hard, he thrust deep inside my pussy making me sing with joy. I love the way he smells, I know this man from somewhere, I know I do, but where? I ask myself. "I want you to fuck me real good, so good that I come back for more." He said.

He put me on the bed on my knees and fucked me from the back, the dick was so good he had me begging for more. My alarm started to go off, and we both jumped at the sound of the noise. Damn I said to myself. He laid me back on the bed and bent down and whispered in my ear, "it was a pleasure as always." He kissed me on the cheek, "don't take off the blindfold until I have left." And then he was gone. I waited for ten minutes before removing the blindfold. I looked around my room and he was nowhere to be found. Again he left a box of chocolate covered strawberries. Getting up I headed for the shower and prepare for work, with a smile on my face. Whom ever he is he can come back any time. I know he will be back again.

As I walked into work and enter my little cubicle I'm feeling better then I had in the past year.

I have a smile on my face, and a new pep to my step. My friend Ashley comes over to my cubicle and ask "what has gotten into you lately? You seem happy, you have a glow about you." I look up at her from my desk and say "I am happy, if all goes the way I plan I will no longer be a single woman."

"Did something happen that you are not telling me? I didn't know that you were seeing anyone." Ashley states. "I'm not really," I say. I see Chad walking by, he looks at me and smiles. For the first time, I really paid attention to him and noticed that he is actually really cute. He has a nice body as well, and he smells… Oh! my gosh it couldn't be… I look at him again and he winked at me and disappeared into the elevator. Later that night as I was watching TV, the news interrupted my program with a special report on 'The Strawberry Bandit'. The news lady reports that the strawberry bandit strikes again, but not like before. "It seems that 'The Strawberry Bandit' has given up on sneaking into women's homes at night while they sleep.

The Strawberry Bandit has been to over fifty homes of single women, and has not been caught by the police. We have come to enjoy the stories of the women who claim to have been visited by this man. His last victim if you can call her a victim was upset that he didn't have sex with her. She said that he left a note with a box of chocolate covered strawberries." They showed the note on the screen, and the reporter read the words to all the viewers,

"I have found the woman of my dreams and I no longer want to satisfy anyone but her." The news lady said. "Well ladies it seems that we have seen the last of the 'Strawberry Bandit.'

Now back to your regularly scheduled program."

I felt sad because I just knew that he was gonna come back, and I thought I knew who 'The Strawberry Bandit' was.

I guess I was wrong. I lay in bed waiting to see if he would show up, but he never did. Walking into work on Friday morning, I head to my cubicle, I find a box with a note on my desk, I look around to see who may have left it there. I open the note,

"I know you didn't sleep well last night, I can fix all that for you if you allow me too.

The Strawberry Bandit."

I looked around the office and the only person I see is Chad coming off the elevator. He looks my way and smiles at me, and keeps on going. No way it just couldn't be him, I say to myself. As the day goes by my mind kept going back to Chad, wondering if the rumors were true about him liking me and, thinking about what it would be like to date him. Because I had a feeling that he left the note on my desk. Later that night as I lie in bed waiting to fall asleep, and hoping that I would get a visit from the 'Strawberry Bandit' again, not realizing that I had fallen asleep. I wake up with a smile on my face, blindfolded and tied to my bed. Oh how I have come to love waking up like this. "You came back." I say to him. "Yes, I came back. You knew that I would, didn't you?"

"I hoped that you would." I told him. He unties my hands and legs, "will you keep the blindfold on until I say you can take it off?" I nod my head yes in response. I feel him lay down on my bed, I lean over him and touch him and just take in his scent, and I think I know who it is but not sure, his voice is familiar but because I never really talked to him at work I can't be sure.

But just laying next to him was like coming home after a long day's work. He turns me over and licks my honey pot from the back, and starts to fuck me hard and fast. This shit felt so good, he licks me from the top of my neck to the middle of my ass crack, sending shivers all over my body.

All the while I keep thinking I know this man from somewhere, because I have smelled this cologne somewhere before. He spreads my butt cheeks and licks me there, my eyes roll to the back of my head the way that he makes me feel inside is just so amazing. "You said once that if I came to visit you, you would fuck me so good, and suck my dick and make me cum every time; so that I don't have to go creeping into other women's window's. Do you remember saying that?" He said softly after eating my ass. I sucked in a deep breath, because there was only two people around when I said that shit. "Yes! I remember saying it." I told him. "Did you mean what you said? Do you want to be the only one for me?"

"Yes." I say to him. "Dana, do you know who I am?" I smile and say, "I've had an idea of who you were the second time you came through my window." He laughs and say "I never came through your window, I came through the front door." He takes the blindfold off, and Like I thought it was Chad the computer tech guy from work.

"Can I be your Strawberry Bandit?" He ask me as he kisses me softly on the lips. "You can most definitely be my Strawberry Bandit." I say with a smile on my face.

Dear Diary (I've been bad)

Dear Diary I was bad today, I really tried to control myself, but the call of the night pulled me out. You see I have this need to fuck sometimes. Sometimes more than one person at a time. I was at the club having a drink and a good time, and I saw him sit down at the bar and looking at me. He wasn't all that hot, but he was dressed nice, and before he sat down I peeped his package. He was built nice also. But at that moment I didn't care, I just wanted some dick tonight. And I just sought out my prey. Now to find me another one to go with this one. Because I'm feeling like a threesome

tonight. I know I should have stayed at home tonight but the urge to fuck was stronger than than the urge to stay at home. So there I was out on the prowl. Well, well, well look who I see coming through the door of the Night Owl. My ex-boyfriend Brad, I smile to myself because I know that me and him have good chemistry, and he would be down with whatever. Brad spots me at the bar, and puts a smile on his face as he walks over to me. We hugged and kissed each other on the cheek. I swear this man gets sexier and sexier as time goes by. With his high yellow fine ass, he has the smallest lips for a man, but can eat pussy like no other.

He is six foot, two inches tall, with a bald head, damn he fine. With arms the size of bricks, and a body that most men try hard to get. And his head game as he called it was on point. Brad is the sweet romantic type of nigga that you settle down with, and he has a scrumptious dick. "What you getting into tonight?" I asked, as he sat down next to me. "Shid hopefully you," he replied with a chuckle, I looked at him and smiled, because he just made my night. Brad knew that I like that wild freaky shit sometimes, there was no game playing with him. Shid because he was into that shit too.

"You must be on the prowl tonight?" He said looking around the club. I took a sip of my Pink Cosmo Punk and lowered my eyes, and smiled at him, "you already know," I said. "So what you feeling like tonight ma?" He asked. "Because I know a place called The Velvet Door Blue, that you can get all your fantasies taken care of or we can have our own little party like in the past."

"Let's do our own thing tonight." I replied. So he called a few of our friends that we use to party with back in the day, then we left the club. Pulling up we see his boys waiting for us, outside his place. Back in the day they were called the Three musketeers,

and I was their sidekick, because we were always together. We did everything together for real. Dion and Brandon gave me hugs, and kisses on the cheek, its been awhile since we all got together and did our thing.

But we knew what it was when we got together. Like they say what we do between us, stays between us. Brad has this room in his basement that he calls his sex cave.

It has everything you need for any kind of sex games, you are into, such as bondage, toys, tables equipped with all kinds of shit. I love this room. I head for the table and climb up on it, Brad lifts my dress up and slides my thong off. I place my feet in the stirrups like at

the doctor's office, and let my legs fall to the side. I like hanging out with these guys because there is no assumptions about anything after we finish our thing, We do what we do and go our separate ways until next time. Dion and Brandon take turns eating my pussy while I work my magic on Brad's dick with my mouth and tongue. Dion straps me to the table and fucks me the way I like it, hard and fast. While I continue to put in work on Brad's pole, Brandon is working on my breast, squeezing and sucking my breast like he is milking a cow, and I love it. He clamps these buds onto my nipples that sends mild shock pulses through my nipples, I cum so

hard from this shit, that my eyes roll to the back of my head. Dion, Brad and Brandon shoots their cum all over me at the same time.

"My turn to pound that pussy," Brad says, as he unhooks me from the table and place me on the floor so that I can't move while he fucks me from behind. You might call me a hoe for doing this with three guys, but I don't see it that way, I see it as four friends enjoying each other sexually. Doing things that no one else can do for you. While Brad is fucking me Dion kneels down in front of me for me to suck him off. Getting fucked hard from behind, and in your mouth, man it is something. Most women couldn't take it, but I've been doing this

shit with them since college. Damn I think to myself this is one of the reasons I'm single. Because no man will be able to do the things that we all do together, Or allow his girl to do these things with someone else. I scream out as Brad smacks me hard on the ass, and I explode all over his dick, while Dion cums in my mouth, and down my throat.

"Damn this some good ass pussy ma," Brad says. Both Dion and Brandon agrees.

"Why is this pussy so good?" I ask them. "Because it knows how to hug a nigga's dick, and it taste like sweet strawberries." Brandon responds. "And yo pussy is like sunshine on a rainy day." Brad adds. "Plus this pussy is just

off the chain, It's juicy all the time." Dion says. I begin to laugh out loud at them, "ya'll crazy," I say to them. As the night went on I got fucked in every way mentionable. But what I loved most was when they all fuck me at the same time. Yeah I know it sounds crazy but I love it when one is in my ass, one in my pussy, and one in my mouth.

All that stimulation at one time is like fireworks in the middle of a blizzard. I have never had sex with Dion and Brandon by themselves. I use to date Brad, but we have always included the other two whenever we wanted to spice things up.

And it's been that way ever since. I don't know why I sometimes have this need to have sex with more than one person sometimes. I think it stems from when I was younger and the older boys use to mess with me and one day when I was coming home from school a group of boys had their way with me, and did all types of things to me. I shake my head to remove the sad memories from my mind, and focus on Brandon taking out the handcuffs and cuffing me to this table that has two dildo's attached to it. One shaped like a child's size fist, and one shaped like a penis.

He spreads my legs open and bends them at the knee and straps my feet down. My pussy and asshole are open wide and exposed. I moved to the edge of the table so that they can insert both dildo's in both holes at the same time. I close my eyes to get adjusted to them being inside me, because the feeling is so different then the real thing. Even though it is battery operated it can sometimes be awkward at first until you get adjusted to the machine. Brad came up with this concept one day when he realized that he could not insert his whole hand in my vagina.

But he loves to watch me take in a fist and a dick at the same time and watch me cum from it. I like it because of the pain and pleasure that I get from having a hand in my pussy and a dick in my ass at the same time.

Brandon turns on the table and the two dildo's slowly start to rotate and pulsate inside me. As they slowly turn up the settings the dildo's start to move in and out, faster and faster, harder and harder. I start to get wetter and wetter. And it goes in and out with ease, as the fist keeps hitting my g-spot and the vibration and stimulation on my clit is making me cum harder than anything before, and I love it... My toes curl and I start to climax from

the force of being fucked by a machine.

Brad squeezes my breast hard and starts to bite my nipples making me scream out in ecstasy as I cum some more. My pussy is dripping wet and running on the floor. Dion is masturbating while watching me being fucked by the machine and cumming all over again and again. He shoots his cum on my stomach. Brandon paused the machine while the dildo's are still inside me, and they start to vibrate, the one in my ass starts to spin like it was drilling for oil, but oh how that shit feels so good.

Brad pulls the dildo's out my ass and pussy, my shit is stretched wide open. My pussy juices is just leaking everywhere. While I'm wide open on the table Brad sits down in front of me and, because this is the only time that he can get his whole hand inside my pussy, he slowly inserts four fingers in me and begins to finger me as he slowly inserts his thumb inside as well, until his whole hand was inside my pussy. He gently closes his hand into a fist I began to slowly fuck his hand and the feeling is unexplainable. My pussy is humming, and my juices are all over his arm. He begins to move his hand in and out, he slowly opens his hand again inside me and begins to rub on my

g-spot, and sending me over the edge. I hear a phone ringing in the background, breaking the flow to my orgasm.

Dion's wife has called, and he has to leave, so we try to continue on with what we were doing because I still need to cum before we all depart. Brad starts to rub that spot again and my legs begin to shake and I can feel my orgasm coming on hard, meanwhile Brandon puts his dick in my mouth, and starts to fuck me in the mouth and hits the back of my throat, Dion puts a strap around the base of my boobs and pulls it tight and puts my breast in his mouth and sucks on them as he begins to

nibble and bite my nipples and breast I arch my back because it just feels so damn good.

"Harder, Do it harder, fuck me harder," I tell them. They do as I say, squeezing my breast harder, fucking me harder until I can't take it any more. I scream out as I release every ounce of cum onto his hands and arm. He slowly removes his hand from inside me and lets me taste my own juices, I savor the taste of me, as Brandon fucks me one last time, and Dion takes his turn in fucking me in the ass... Brad unstrapped me from the table and helps me up, I proceed to the shower in the basement to clean up before I leave, I hug and

kiss them goodbye. Brad takes me back to my car and I go on my way…

Dear Diary I've been bad. But I can't wait for the next time we get together. Because being bad is sometimes a good thing.

Unsatisfied

Dear Diary, 3/15/2001

Sitting at my desk at work, my mind started to wander to the night at the club,where I met Romeo. I don't even know his last name. It don't matter because he was a one night stand for me anyway. And honestly he wasn't all that great. I don't even know what made me have sex with him. As I enter my daily thoughts in my journal for the day, I come out of my day dreaming when I hear my phone ring on my desk. "Yes?" I answer, "you have a call on line

one." My secretary tells me. "Thank you. This is Lisa, how may I help you?" I asked when I clicked on line one. After my phone call with my client, I decided to go out for lunch, to finish my daily journal logs. While at lunch I had the urge to have sex. Why? I don't know. ever since my husband and I split a year and a half ago, I have not been able to find anyone to satisfy my sexual needs, or my need to have to sex constantly; So here I am having these sexual quest to try and satisfy my sexual needs. There are times that I have had sex with three or more guys a day, I'm just so unsatisfied.

I run into an old friend of mine from college, while going to lunch, we end up having lunch together. during our lunch conversation, she tells me about this place called 'The Velvet Door Blue.' But you can only get in by invite only, she said. She also told me that it's a place where you can go have all you fantasies fulfilled. And no one knows who you are, because the rules are that you have to wear a mask at all times. But once you get the invite they give you the option to become a V.I.P member, you pay an annual fee and go as much or as little as you want.

This is somewhere I need to go, I tell her, how I can't control this need that I have to have sex all the time. We ate our lunch, then we said our goodbye's and promised to keep in touch. On my way back to the office I ran into a guy I use to have sexual relations with, He had a big dick, and knew how to use it, and eat pussy, so of course I asked what he was about to get into because I really needed to have sex at that moment. Even if it was a quickie. He was also on his lunch break, and he was feeling the way I was at the moment. Good thing he lived close by.

At his condo, before we could get inside good I had his pants unzipped, and his dick out, he closed the door behind us and I dropped to my knees so that I could put his big long hard dick in my mouth.

I sucked him so good and hard that he came quick as fuck. As I swallowed his cum I worked his dick some more, putting it deeper and deeper down my throat.

Damn I can remember this as if it was today.

I laugh to myself, as I continue documenting my thoughts and indiscretions in my journal. I could hear him moaning as he pulls my head

hard onto his dick forcing it down my throat even more. I take his balls and gently place them in my mouth as I stroke his dick from tip to shaft, gently squeezing the tip of the head, he pulls me up off my knees, turns me around to face the door, pulls up my skirt, sees that I have no panties on and pushes his dick inside me from the back. pushes his dick inside me from the back.

There's pain but it quickly turns to pleasure as he pounds my pussy from the back.

Damn this shit is good I say to myself.

Dear Diary, *why am I so unsatisfied? I ask as I pause to reflect on some things going on in my life. I realize that it all stems from a lack of self esteem, I shake my head and continue writing. As I lean into the door with my ass pushed out, he took his dick out and turned me around and pushed me back up against the door and bends down to eat my pussy, biting me on the thighs, my pussy lips, and biting my clit gently. Standing up he begins to kiss me. I could taste my own juices on his lips as we kiss. This turns me on even more, tasting my own juices.*

I put my fingers to my clit and squeeze, Chris pulled me from the door, walked me towards his bedroom.

He removed our clothes, pushing me onto the bed, with my back facing him, he pulls me up on my knees by my waist. With my ass in the air, he spreads my cheeks as he eats my juicy pink pussy, and licks my ass from behind. I came so hard and fast that it ran down my legs onto his bed. I don't know why I love having my pussy ate from behind, but I love it.

It's something about it that makes me want to cum over and over again.

My friends and family thinks that I just need to go and get back with my husband because I didn't have these issues before we split. But Diary how does one go back to someone when they have broken your spirit?

That is a question I will leave unanswered for now. Now back to my journal; Chris sat on the bed and I sat on his dick and rode the shit out his dick. I felt him about to cum again, so I got up and took him in my mouth again, and sucked the cum from his dick until there was nothing left.

Chris flipped me over and put my legs behind my head and climbed on top and

shoved his dick in my ass, and fucked me like that for ten minutes. I was not ready for that. He took his right hand and put two, then three fingers in my vagina stretching it to get four fingers in, he began to massage my G-spot.

I came from him fucking me in the ass and him massaging my G-spot, my body shook from the force of my orgasm. And for a split second I thought that maybe he could be the one to tame my sexual needs and desires. Wishful thinking I guess.

End of entry. 3/16/2001

Back at work.

The next day on my way to my office the receptionist out front tells me that my boss is waiting for me in my office. Damn I say under my breath, I forgot to turn in my quarterly report before I left the office the previous day.

I walk into my office and see Mr. Washington, sitting in one of the chairs in front of my desk. Mr. Washington is an older white guy, in his late forties, he was not bad looking for his age, he's nicely built, with deep grey eyes and jet black hair.

He stands up as I enter my office, "Hi, Lisa, how are you today?" He asked. "I'm wonderful, and you sir?" He looks at me kinda funny and says, "things could be better. I came for your report." I walk to my desk and lean over it to pick up the report for him. Now I have a nice shape if I do say so myself, small waist, big round apple booty and nice perky breast not too small and not too big. As I stand back up I notice that Mr. Washington is staring at my ass. I clear my throat to get his attention, he looks at me and ask me how my pussy taste?

I was taken aback for a second, because he has never came at me like that before nor has he ever came to my office before, or spoken to me except in meetings or in passing. He walks over to my door and locks it and comes back towards me and asks me again, "Lisa how does that pussy taste? Don't worry this is between me and you, I have wanted to know how that pussy tasted since you started working here three years ago."

I looked at him and then the door, and back at him and my pussy started to get wet, from the sheer thought of fucking my boss, and having him under my thumb or wrapped around my finger.

He walked towards me snatched me up by my wrist. I fell into his chest and he put his hands in my hair pulling my head back. As he walked me backwards towards my desk and pushing the papers off to the other side of my desk.

He leaned me back onto my desk and pulled my blouse up, and pulled out one of my breast and put his pink lips on my large buds, he gently sucked and nibbled on it until it was hard as a rock. He leaned down and took my left foot and placed it in one of the chairs in front of my desk and did the same with my right foot leaving my pink pussy fully exposed for him to see.

He started to lick his lips and shake his head as he ran his left hand down my pussy lips, stopping at the entrance of my love cave. Parting my pussy lips open, with one hand and licking his fingers on the other hand, he slowly inserted a finger, then two turning them around in my pussy, my shit began to throb like crazy.

Damn, I thought to myself, this muthafucka got my pussy throbbing overtime. He closes his eyes as he removes his fingers and bring them to his lips to taste my essence, I began to moan out loud. I knew that I had him when he began to moan also, because I know this pussy of mine has that effect on men and women a like.

"Oh, Lisa can, I please put my mouth on this hot ass juicy pussy of yours?" He asked. I looked at him and said "if you eat this, pussy I want a raise and a better office, and another week of vacation." He looked at me, "only if your pussy taste as good as the juices on my fingers did." I laughed out loud and said, "then you better put that into effect before you walk out my office." He bent down and put his mouth on my love cave, and tasted my honey, my eyes rolled to the back of my head, as my boss licked and sucked and bit down on this juicy ass pussy.

I began to squirt in his mouth, and shake uncontrollably on my office desk; I could feel his tongue and his fingers inside my pussy. I felt him press his thumb at the entrance of my back door, and slowly insert it inside.

"Oh! Damn" I whisper out loud, "this shit feels good, oh so good," as I moan out loud.

Mr. Washington bites my clit very gently sending shivers through my body. As the last few spasms leave my body he lifts his head up from between my legs and wipes his mouth, he smiles at me, "that was the best tasting pussy that I've had in a long...Very long time."

He takes my legs out of the chairs and stands me up right and fixes my clothes, then reaches across my desk and picks up my report. He opens the door and walks out, closing the door behind him. I paced my office floor, trying to

wrap my head around what just happened here in my office with my boss. I take the rest of the day off because after that I just could not function. I went home to shower and changed into my workout clothes, I had to work out clear my head.

Dear Diary, I am very confused right now, because this white man sure knows how to eat some pussy right.

And for the first time in a long time I don't want to have sex with anyone else. And he didn't even fuck me, he just ate my pussy to the fullest. End of entry: 3/17/2001

The next morning when I arrived at work walking towards my office the receptionist stops me and says, "Ms. Lisa that is no longer your office," with a frown on her face. I stop in my tracks and walk over to her desk, "what do you mean not my office anymore?, have I been terminated and not notified?" I say to her, as my voice starts to rise. "No, no, no Mr. Washington placed you on the third floor in one of the offices up there.

You got a promotion as well, that report must have been something." She said.

As I get on the elevator to go up to my new office on the third floor, I had a big smile on my face, because I knew why and how this all happened. Juicy has done it again... I laugh out loud. Exiting the elevator on the third floor, Mr. Washington is waiting for me in the hallway, "Hello, Lisa, how are you this morning?" he asks. "Well good morning Mr. Washington, how are you this fine morning?" I replied . He walks me to my new office and shows me around, "wow this is beautiful," I tell him. "Thank you very much."

He walks me to my new desk and sat me down in the huge leather chair behind it, he walked back across the room and locked the door. With his long stride, he made it back to me in six steps. He swung my chair around to face him, he placed his hands on both sides of the chair, "Lisa, all I could think about last night was the taste of your juicy pussy, it had me up all night, had me going crazy thinking about tasting it again and again and again. I want to know can I please taste it again?"

"I have never been with a woman of color before, but I find you to be very beautiful, and I have always wanted you.

He leans in and kisses me softly on the lips, sucking my bottom lip into his mouth, and gently biting it. Damn this white man can kiss. I have never been with a white man, or even wanted to be with one, but this man here. oh wee he can get it. I laugh at myself for thinking this, but at the same time I'm serious. I kiss him back, like I was trying to make him mine, but maybe in the back of my head I was. He rubs his hands all over my body making me want him even more, and I could feel the wetness forming between my legs. I knew this was gonna happen and I was prepared for it, because juicy was the bomb dot com.

I looked at my boss as I spread my legs wide for him to see that I wore no panties under my black and white maxi dress with matching jacket, that stopped at my waist with one button to keep it closed, and showed off my small waist. Mr. Washington bent down on his knees and just looked at my open pussy as if he could not wait to be inside her. He looked at me and asked me could he feel me too. Even though I love dick, every once in awhile I let a female eat out the honey pot, but I have never let a white man get close to my honey pot until now, but then again, I already knew that I was gonna fuck my boss.

"Please, Lisa, can I feel you?" I didn't answer him, I just took him by the head and slowly pulled him towards juicy. Yes my pussy has a name, because she gets very juicy all the time. He began to stick his tongue inside juicy and twirl it around, he spread my lips apart and sucked on each one, tilting my chair back and pulling me closer to his mouth.

My pussy started letting her juices flow over his tongue, as he slurped and sucked my honey from its pot.

I moaned at the way he ate my pussy. He stood up and unzipped his pants pulling out his large love stick, with a big head and thick ass shaft. I watched as it pulsated in front of me, I took it in my hands and guided it into my mouth. I knew that he would enjoy it and so would I. I could tell by the way his head fell back that he was enjoying this dick sucking. I felt him contracting and I knew he was about to cum, and I was ready to take it all. Never have I tasted cum so sweet like he had been eating fruit all week. I sucked every drop of cum from his big dick.

They say white men have small dicks, well this is proof that white or black, they all come in small, medium and large. Mr. Washington was very blessed in that department. I saw the tension leave his shoulders as he dropped to the floor and put his face back between my legs. He took a big whiff of my essence as he pulled me from the chair and turned me around and slowly pushed my head into the seat of the chair, leaving my ass in the air and my love tunnel open. He pushed his tongue inside me from the back, he sucked on my lips so hard that I came, spreading my ass cheeks open, he fucked me in the ass with his tongue.

He reached up onto the desk and grabbed a big black cone shaped statue, that I didn't even notice was there. He slowly inserted it into my wet pussy and began moving it in and out slowly. "How does that feel Lisa? Do you like that in your pussy?" I didn't know what to say at first because I have never used objects in my pussy before. But as I got used to it being there, he started to fuck me faster and faster with it, I can't believe that I was starting to enjoy this shit and wanted more. "More, I want more," I said to him. He stood up and pushed his love stick in my ass, while he fucked me with the statue as well.

With him in my ass, and the statue in my pussy, I started to tremble all over and I was releasing all my juices on the statue and the floor. "More," I said, as he fucked me harder and harder with his dick and the statue.

Never in my life have I enjoyed sex like this, he pulled the statue out and licked my juices from it. He replaced the statue back on my desk, pulled his dick out my ass, he walked to a door to the right of my desk and went inside, coming back with a warm rag and small hand towel. He cleaned me off and then himself, fixed my clothes and his, he then kissed me on the lips and neck as he

hugged me, then he turned towards the door.

He pointed to the statue and said, "don't use that without me." He opened the door and walked out my office, shutting the door behind him.

Dear Diary, ***my pussy still throbs and aches every time I think about this between me and Mr. Washington. This went on with my boss for a year. And every time my pussy just got juicer and juicer. And for once I am no longer unsatisfied.... I am now Mrs. Washington. Happy and satisfied.***

End of entry: 4/12/2002

Fantasizing

I watch you every day and I fantasize about the Things I want you to do to me, and with me. I watch you look at at me and I know that you don't know the kinds of things that goes on in my mind- like touching your body all over.

I fantasize about making love to you, in the park, under the stars and the moon. I wonder if you knew that I love how your skin smells after you have been working all day. I fantasize about your lips on my breast, as you bite, and squeeze my nipples, and breast.

I often wonder what you would think if you knew that I fantasized about you fucking me from behind, as you pull my head back by my hair and kiss me as you stare into my eyes. I often fantasized about the way you touched my body as you fucked me harder and harder.

I wonder do you know that I've watched you as you work, as you walked down the aisle way. I see you looking at me while your working, and I wonder are you fantasizing about me too. Do you have the same things going through your mind as I do. I think about how it would be if you were to kiss me.

When I see your smile I think about your lips on my pussy and tasting my wetness. What would you do if you knew the things that I fantasize about? Would you accept the offer of me wanting to give myself to you? would you smile and walk away from what I have to offer, I wonder what you would do if you knew. I smile at the thought of you finding out. I fantasize about you fucking me while I sit on your lap, with a crowd of people walking by, and not knowing what we are doing. I wonder what you would do... I've wondered do you fantasize about fucking me too, or pulling my head back by my hair and asking me is this

pussy yours, as you thrust your dick inside my pussy. I wonder if you would allow me to straddle your face so you can fuck me with your tongue. I fantasize about all kinds of things I would like you to do, like tie me up and have your way with me. I fantasize about hearing you say take this dick, all of it. and feeling your cum shoot all over me. Damn! my pussy is wet. I can see you between my legs looking at me as you drink the last drops of my juices, uh, mmm that feels so good. I wonder how you would feel inside me as you grow harder and harder. I wonder does your cum taste sweet like strawberries, or watermelon

on a hot summer night. Damn boy you got me all hot and bothered, I touch myself wishing it was your hands on me, touching squeezing, groping, and slapping his ass of mine. I imagine how big you are as you slide in and out of me. I've watched you watching me from afar, are you thinking what I'm thinking? I think about how you would react if I walked up to you and ran my hands down your arms.

I wonder what you are thinking right now. I can see you kissing me on the ass and gently biting me on my legs, my back, my arms, my thighs and my ass, as you stream kisses all over my body.

Damn! I wish I knew what you were thinking right now as you watch me work. I fantasize about you walking up behind me and gently brush your dick along my ass, or wrapping your arms around me, and pinching me softly on the nipples, until my pussy begins to get wet. Would you get on your knees and and spread my legs open and eat my pussy from behind, Would you? I see you watching me from across the way, you have that look in your again; are you fantasizing about what I'm fantasizing about? Mmm... I wonder what you think about when you watch me.

Do you see me licking my lips and ruining my hands over my breast while you watched me from over there? Do you fantasize about touching me there between my legs and tasting my essence? I see you smile at me as I walk by you, and gently touch your hand when no one is looking. But most of all I see how you look at me when you think I'm not watching.

Tell me what are you thinking when you look at me? Do you think about driving somewhere out the way and touching me all over?

Or do you think about watching me masturbate in front of you? I fantasize about those things all day long when I see you walking by.

It's a damn shame that all I can do is fantasize about the way I want you to fuck me, touch me and taste me. But oh how I love to fantasize about you. I love it when you lick your lips when you smile at me, yeah I know you see it too, the way I put an extra shimmy in my walk when you're around.

Damn I want to taste you so bad, uh, ooh, mmm, boy it's a damn shame how you make me want you so much just from watching you from across the way. But damn I love fantasizing about you.

Be Careful What You Wish For

It started four months ago when I was feeling down about myself. It seemed like everything was against me. I hated the people that I worked with, I had lost my boyfriend of ten years to a younger woman six months before this. And not only that I started to gain weight. I was feeling depressed. All this happened within a span of a year.One day four months ago while at work I was taking a call from a client and before I could hang up from the call, my client says to me "be careful what you wish for, because it may not be what you really want or need in your life."

I looked at the phone and before I could respond the line went dead, now I'm saying to myself what the hell was that all about, and how do they know what I have been wishing for. After I prepare to leave for home at the end of my shift I decide to stop and get me a bottle of Pink Moscato to have with my dinner tonight. It was nothing fancy just some leftover hamburger helper, the crunchy taco kind. You see I use to cook big meals for my man and I when I had one, but lately I just haven't done it much.

As I walk into my house off of Philadelphia Dr. and Marlay, I kick off my wedges and start my process of removing my work clothes as I head to my bedroom. As I'm walking to my room I notice that a light is on, and I know that had turned it off before I went into work that morning.

I paid it no mind, thinking I may have forgotten to turn it off again. Now mind you this was the third time that week that I have found that light on when I got home from work. I continue on with my routine of taking a shower and fixing my dinner and getting ready for the next day.

But this day was different, I felt it when I walked through my door that something was different in my house. It felt like someone was watching me, every once in awhile it would feel like someone or something rubbed up against me… but no one was there. I ate my dinner and drank my bottle of Moscato… Yes the whole bottle by myself. After the news goes off I head back to my room for bed, again I feel someone watching me, so I go and check my house one last time, again nothing. Now I don't know about you but I sleep in the nude, so as I take my lounge clothes off I feel something touch my pussy so I look down, and again nothing is there.

I say to myself "girl you are really trippin, or you need some good dick in yo life, cause you imaging shit." Before I get in the bed I say my nightly prayers. I pray for my family and friends and I always at the end throw in --" and please send me some good dick, Amen." So on that night something or someone heard my plea.

In the middle of the night I was awakened by someone sucking my breast and fingers in my pussy, I thought I was dreaming at first, because when I looked there was no one there. I lie back down waiting to see if it would happen again, nothing.

"Damn!" I say to myself, that shit sure as hell felt good. I go back to sleep and again I feel someone licking my pussy and sucking my breast, I don't wake up because I don't want it to stop. Next thing I know I feel my legs being spread apart, and I keep my eyes shut because it feels so good. I really don't want it to stop.

In all my adult life my pussy never felt like that, it has never been eaten like that. It felt like it was being eaten from the inside out. This went on all night long, and all of a sudden it just stops. All I can do is let the tears run down my face, as I say out loud, "please don't stop, please don't stop…"

my alarm clock goes off and I wake up. Damn what a dream, I shower and get dressed for work. Shit I have a smile on my face, cause the dream I had the night before had me feeling like-- damn!. I had a little pep in my step that day, and I couldn't wait to get off work so I could get back to my dream. Later that night after work I get a call from my girl LaShawnda, she wanted to see how I was feeling, because she knew that I had been feeling down and out lately. "Girl, I feel good today, had the bomb ass dream last night," I told her. She laughed at me and said, "girl, you really need some good dick in yo life, that kind that leaves you drained in the morning and

sapped of energy." I co-sign with her, "I know that's right honey, I need that good, good shit that keeps you in the bed for days at a time," I say laughing into the phone. We talked a little while longer, said our goodbyes and I love yous and hung up. Again I go through my daily routine of showering and eating dinner and drinking my Moscato. As I'm eating I say out loud "damn I wish I had some good, good dick that kind that leaves you spent and keeps you in bed for days."

Again I feel someone watching me as I prepare for bed, this time I don't even care, because I

just want to get to sleep so I can have my dream again. Like the night before. I feel hands all over my body, squeezing my breast, sucking on my breast. I feel hands on my ass squeezing and biting me all over. I open my eyes because it feels so real that it can't be a dream. But yet again there is no one there. I look down and the sheets to my bed are gone, and I still feel hands on my body. Now I'm scared because I know that I'm awake, at least I think I'm awake. I can't help but like and enjoy what is happening to me. I don't want it to stop.

Again this goes on all night, and suddenly stops, right before my alarm goes off. I don't know what to make out of what happened last night. By Friday morning I didn't know if I would make it through the day without passing out. I couldn't wait to get home that night ,not for the sex but to get some sleep.

By the time I got home from work I was too tired to drink my Moscato or eat my dinner, all I could do was shower and fall into bed. When I woke up I knew for sure that I was not dreaming because what was happening to me felt like I had the biggest dick ever inside me, it felt so good and painful at the same time.

I see my breast being sucked and bitten on, but no one was there to do it. I looked down and saw that my arms and legs were tied to the bed, but no rope was visible, and I was spread eagle for the whole world to see.

How the hell did this happen? I know I didn't tie myself up. I started to scream but my scream was stopped by what felt like a dick being shoved into my mouth, but there was no one there to do it.

All I could do was suck it like my life depended on it. Because at that moment I felt like it did. It felt like there was a dick in every available hole big enough to fit one in.

Never had I been fucked in my ass before, like that, but whatever was doing this to me had me on my knees now fucking me in my ass so hard and fast, I thought I would pass out. All the while I have a dick in my pussy, and my mouth. Something was sucking and squeezing my breast, all at the same time. And there was no damn body there in the room but me.

I didn't care about screaming anymore, because it felt so damn good by this time, that I didn't care what this thing was doing to me.

This thing finally showed itself to me and when I tell you I felt like crying, I just wanted

to die, because I knew that no one would ever believe me if I told them. It was a spirit of some kind, all I know is that it had me pent up all weekend long. It would not let me eat, drink shower or go to the restroom. All I know is that it was the most pleasurable and the most painfullest weekend ever. On Sunday night it suddenly stopped, as if nothing had ever happened. My body was bruised and sore all over, from all the things that it had done to me. Have you ever heard that saying 'I fucked her until she couldn't walk.' Well that literally happened to me I had to call off work for a

week just so that I could recover from my weekend-- of what I don't know. I had no energy or the willpower to get out my bed to shower and eat. So for a week I stayed in my bed, with no sign of my nightly visitor. I didn't know if I should be happy or sad for that.

***MONDAY** morning when I returned to work my friend called me and wanted to know why I didn't answer my phone all weekend or the previous weekend. "Hell you wouldn't believe me if I told you." I replied.*

Later that night at home I was hoping to get into bed and get some rest, like the previous week, but that was not the case. My visitor came back every night for a month and fucked me endlessly every night. One night I was literally on the wall as it fucked me so good and hard, it felt like it was trying to kill me. But I couldn't stop enjoying how my pussy would get so wet, and my orgasms kept

coming and coming. Or how it's dick tasted so damn good to me, and how being fucked in my ass became my favorite thing to do. Or how it sucked my breast so good it was painful. I just couldn't get enough of how it ate my pussy and my ass, it felt like it was sticking its tongue in one hole and out the other.

Because I haven't had any good sex in so long I couldn't stop enjoying it... But what I didn't know was that it was literally killing me slowly, it was sucking the energy right out my body. With every hard pump in my pussy or my ass it was sucking the life out of me.

Every time it put its dick in my mouth it was choking the life out of me. I felt my body going limp, but all I could think about was how good this shit felt and didn't want it to end, at least not yet. All of a sudden my body hit the floor and everything just stopped. I woke up in the hospital. I could not explain the bruises all over my body, or tell anybody what I had been through for the past two months. LaShawnda came to see me, and she tells me about a dream she had and feeling like it was the best sex ever.

I closed my eyes because I knew what she was feeling and what she was about to endure for the next several months or longer depending on how long it wants to use her…I looked at her and said, "be careful of what you wish for, because it may not be what you want or need in your life." And I pray for my friend, because I know that it's more than just a dream, and more to life than good Dick…

Coming Soon...

Never Should've Loved Him

NJS BOOKS

I felt like he was placing me under some kind of a spell or hypnotizing me...

The tingling sensation in Jessica's body was a feeling that she had not felt in a long ass time. "Your pussy is so damn good Jessica, I don't want to stop eating it." That made her pussy wetter than it was. "This pussy is so damn juicy and wet, daaamn, how this pussy gets so wet like this?" He asked and all Jessica could do was moan in response. Greg began to tease her for a while, she hated when he did this. "Why are you teasing me?" Jessica asked. "Teasing is pleasing and you deserve to be teased."

Chapter One

Jessica Sighed and drank the rest of her drink. "I know Lynne; it's as if I live my life the same way everyday as before. Even my weekends are boring and predictable as hell. I hope my life will not always be this damn boring…bland." Lynne looked at her sister as if she was crazy or something. "Jessica, you're only forty-four girl, your kids are grown and on their own. If you feel like your life is so boring, do something about it. Get out and meet new people, get a new hobby or something."

Jessica shrugged. "I've done that already. I go line dancing on Wednesdays at the Fox Trot

lounge. Sometimes I feel as if I just don't fit in anywhere." Lynne picked up her check to pay on the way out. "I don't know what to say Jessica, you've always been a loner by nature, but you've got to open yourself up more. Get out and get a new man or something." Jessica followed Lynne out of Ray's Chicken and Fish restaurant and rolled her eyes at her sister as they got into the car. Getting a new man was easy for Lynne, but not for Jessica. In addition, a new man was not the solution to the problem at hand. "Finding a good man isn't easy Lynne. Not for me anyway." Lynne shook her head. "You shouldn't sell yourself short, Jessica you're a beautiful woman. You still look young, and you do not need makeup to look good. "I'm envious of you, for real."

Jessica rolled her eyes and laughed. "Girl you are not envious of me." "Quit, Jessica you have a nice body, you've lost weight since you've been line dancing. However, you are still a work in progress. It will take some time to get where you want to be. Plus Rome wasn't built in a day." Jessica hit Lynne in the arm, "fuck you Lynne, but I love you anyway. Don't know what I would do without you."

Don't know what I would do without you."

"I don't know either. Anywho back to your boring life. "Yeah, and what about it?" Lynne laughed. "You need a vacation."

The light changed and they drove down the street. "I don't know, it's been a long time, some years since I had a vacation."

"Where did you go on your last vacation?"

"Disney World."

Lynne looked at her with a disgusted look on her face. "You mean to tell me that your last vacation was some years ago and it was with the kids at Disney World? Jessica shrugged. "It was a family vacation for a few weeks. "Lynne shook her head and drove on. "Girl you need to get your sexy ass on a plane and go somewhere new, someplace warm and tropical, someplace exciting." "Like where?" Jessica asked. She always had a problem with making decisions about doing anything for herself. If left up to her, she would not go on a vacation. Lynne shrugged. "I don't know, how about you write down six places you would like to go visit. Put them in a bowl and pick one.

It shouldn't matter where you go, since your life is as boring as you say." "That actually sounds like fun. When I get home I will do just that."Lynne rolled her eyes. "Yeah right."

Jessica hated when people doubted her, even her sister. "Okay, you'll see." Lynne dropped Jessica off at home, getting out of the car; she hugged her sister, and dreading going into her lonely house.

At that moment, she decided to take a much-needed vacation, and she would take a chance on the destination by picking it out of a bowl.

Jessica's dream of owning her own business was finally happening. She was weeks away from starting a new life and new business. Jessica wiped the frown off her face and

thought she would show her sister that she could be adventurous after all.

Later that night, Jessica put six pieces of paper in a bowl with the places she wanted to go on her vacation. The list of potential places was random, although Jessica did a good job of picking the destinations all over the country. Some of the places were just places on her bucket list to visit one day.

However, she planned to be true to whatever she picked. No matter what she picked, she would book her trip to start in the next three weeks. She will put in her vacation time at work the following night.

Now all that is left is to pick the destination for her vacation. "Here we go." Jessica shook the bowl mixing up the folded pieces of paper inside.

She reached in three times to grab a piece of paper and each time she pulled back. She felt it was not quite the right time to gamble.
She took a deep breath, and closed her eyes and just grabbed a piece of paper.

"Let it be Vegas! Please let it be Vegas!"

Chapter 2

North Carolina

Jessica sighed and made a silent prayer. North Carolina was one of the last places she added to the list. She knew little about North Carolina except that Myrtle Beach and her cousin Amber were down that way.

Oh well, the city was on the list and Jessica said she would promise to honor the results. In addition, it had advantages. There was a beach, some sightseeing, tours shopping. Most of all she could spend time with her cousin Amber. She called to let her cousin know that she would be visiting in a few weeks, so that she would be looking out for her arrival.

Jessica arrived at the airport in North Carolina, June tenth at one o'clock in the afternoon. Her cousin Amber was there to meet her. They exchanged hugs and kisses on the cheek. Amber was excited that Jessica had come to visit her in N.C. and would be staying for three weeks. Even though Amber had to work, she still had plans for them to hang out.

Amber took Jessica to her hotel 'The Sea Crest Oceanfront Resort' where she would stay for the next three weeks of her vacation. "Jessica I will pick you up later after you have settled in." "That will be cool, Amber, I'll be ready."

"You do know that you are welcome to stay with me in my guest room?" Amber asked her. Jessica hugged her cousin Amber and laughed. "I know Amber but I didn't want to put you out or anything. Because I know you have to work and all, and this way I can get out on my own and enjoy the town some."

Jessica was relaxing by the pool at her hotel when she saw someone who looked familiar to her. Someone she has not seen in twenty years. She watched as this person walked back into the hotel.

"No it couldn't be, not the Greg Randall," Jessica said in a whisper. Damn the brother was still fine. She thought, Jessica started fantasizing about the time she and Greg had spent together all those years ago. How those were the best times of her life.

She soon came back to reality, because he broke up with her to be with someone else, she thought to herself.

Greg was not for sure if what he saw was real or if his imagination was playing tricks on him. He could have sworn he saw Jessica sitting in one of the lounge chairs out by the pool.

It couldn't have been her he thought, not after twenty years. The love of his life just could not be staying in the same hotel as he. Greg went to his room with Jessica on his mind. Greg thought about the last time they were together how much he has really missed Jessica, and how he had searched for her, to get her back so many years ago.

He thought how he could have been so stupid to let her go, so long ago.

Greg chuckled as he made a shot of 1800 Silver in his room. As the burn of his drink went down his throat, he closed his eyes and remembered the way Jessica smelled, felt and the way she tasted. With a smile on his face, he put down his glass, and hopped in the shower to cool down from all the tantalizing memories that flooded his mind with feelings he thought were gone for Jessica...

ABOUT THE AUTHOR

I am a wife to a hot and sexy man, and mother of two boys and a girl. I have two grandchildren who I love dearly. I am the oldest of a brother and three sisters I grew up in Dayton Ohio, but got to do a little traveling as a kid as my father was in the service. My hobbies include cooking, baking, reading and spending time with my family and friends. I have always had a passion for books, my first real paying job was in a Library, I could sit and read books for hours at a time and recall everything that I read from any book that I have ever read.